Anne of Green Gables

Illustrated by Alan Marks

Based on the novel by L. M. Montgomery
Retold by Mary Sebag-Montefiore

Anne had been an orphan ever since she could remember, but now Matthew and Marilla had agreed to adopt her.

She gazed with delight at the blossoming cherry trees as Matthew drove her to their farm.

"Prince Edward Island is the prettiest place in the world,"
she chattered. "I never thought I'd actually live here.
I can't believe I have a real new..."

"...HOME! Green Gables is just beautiful.
I'd be perfectly happy, if it wasn't for my red hair."

She sighed. "Oh Matthew, red hair is such a trial..."

"It doesn't matter how you look," declared Marilla, when she said goodnight that evening. "Just behave and we'll do our best for you."

"I'll try," came Anne's muffled voice. "But it's really, really hard to be good all the time."

The next morning, Anne looked out from her bedroom window, filled with determination. “Now I’m at Green Gables, I’ll be dazzlingly good always,” she promised.

But that very afternoon, Marilla's friend came for tea.

"Well!" she exclaimed. "What an ugly, skinny child. And her hair's as orange as carrots."

"I HATE YOU!" Anne screamed. "You HORRIBLE woman!"

Furious, Marilla sent Anne
straight to bed.

"You should have heard her
Matthew. Such a temper. What
are we going to do?"

"I'll talk to her,"
Matthew offered, "and
ask her to say sorry."

He found Anne sobbing her heart out.

"I will say sorry," she sniffed. "But only because it's you
asking me Matthew. You and I are kindred spirits."

Anne sank to her knees before Marilla's friend and clasped her hands.

"You were right. I am red haired and ugly.
Please forgive a poor, homeless, unloved orphan."

Marilla couldn't help smiling.
Anne was actually enjoying her apology.

"No house with Anne in it will ever be dull,"
she told Matthew. "I just hope she doesn't
lose her temper at school."

Anne loved school.

Her best friend was Diana, who had shining black hair and dresses with wonderful puffed sleeves.

How Anne longed for a pretty dress too. Her tunics were plain and dull.

"Guess who wants to be your friend?" Diana giggled, one day. "Gilbert Blythe!"

Anne thought Gilbert was cheeky.
She ignored him until he whispered, "Hey, Carrots!"
Then... **THWACK!**

Anne whacked her slate on his head.

"ANNE SHIRLEY!" shouted the teacher.
Anne had to stand in front of her class for the entire afternoon.

She was too angry to cry.
Instead she decided to change her hair.

And she vowed she would
NEVER, EVER, EVER
forgive Gilbert Blythe.

MISS SHIRLEY
HAS A VERY BAD
TEMPER.

When Anne didn't come down for tea, Marilla went to look for her. "You've got green hair!" she gasped.

"I dyed it," Anne wailed, "and it went wrong."

“Oh Matthew, I’m in the depths of despair,” Anne declared the next day. “I didn’t think ANYTHING could be worse than red hair.”

“Cheer up,” Matthew smiled. “It will wash out eventually.”

Anne's hair was soon red again,
as red as the turning leaves, but she didn't mind.

She spent every day with Diana,
sharing stories and sweet ripe apples in the orchard...

...and racing through the frosty winter snows.

For Christmas, Matthew surprised her
with the prettiest dress she had ever seen...

...and she wore it to perform in the school play.

She had never been so happy,

but she still wouldn't forgive Gilbert
for teasing her about her hair.

One afternoon, Anne decided to take out the old boat.

"I'll float off into the far blue yonder..." she murmured.

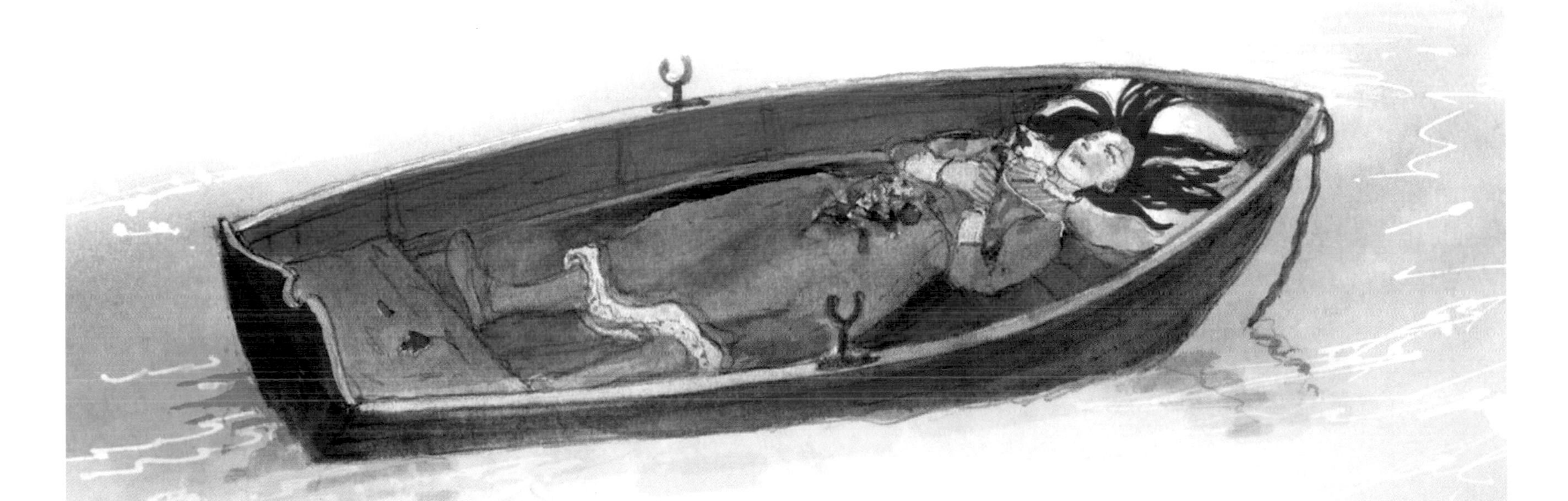

She was drifting in the deepest part of the river,
when the boat sprang a leak.

Anne was lost in a sea of daydreams.
She didn't notice water filling the boat...

"HELP!" she yelled, as she almost capsized.

"Anne?" called a voice. There was Gilbert, pulling her to safety. "I'm sorry I called you Carrots. Can we be friends?"

Anne and Gilbert became the very best of friends.

And when they grew up, they married –
but that's another story...

The "Anne" books

"Anne of Green Gables" was followed by another five books describing Anne's adventures as she grew up, went to college, married Gilbert and raised her large family. Anne appears in several other books, too, though these are mainly about her family and friends.

Edited by Lesley Sims
Designed by Lenka Hrehova

First published in 2016 by Usborne Publishing Ltd., Usborne House, 83-85 Saffron Hill, London EC1N 8RT, England. www.usborne.com First published in America in 2016. UE.